The World's Greatest Invention

By K.C. Pomponio

To any kid who is brave enough to chase their dreams...

Chapter One

Natalie Ornett had me in a daze from the first time I saw her. Brown hair, puppy dog eyes, and a comforting smile. Her locker was just three away from mine in the eight grade hallway. Sometimes, I would give her a glance, but most of the time, I played it cool. Even if my heart was leaping out of my chest and running laps around the gym, I typically wouldn't say much. Besides, I was perfectly fine with staying to myself and going through the motions in my day to day school life. What would I say to her anyway? She seemed like the type of girl that wasn't allowed to date until she was sixteen.

If you asked me, I would say my parents weren't too strict when it came to girls. Well, let me put it this way. Up until eight grade, I had yet to bring a girl home to my family. My guess is they didn't expect me to venture into unknown territory. When I was joking around outside with my friends, girls that went to our school came up during the conversation every now and then. And I could tell from the way my friends talked about girls that they had some growing up to do.

It happened on a Tuesday morning. I was late getting to school, and was one of maybe three kids walking through the poster-lined hallways of Steezberry Middle School.

"Mr. Venezio, are you aware that the first period began seventeen minutes ago?" Mr. Rodriguez, my school principal, quizzed me.

"Yeah, um, I actually just got out of the restroom," I answered him in a modest tone.

Mr. Rodriguez paused to give me a confused look.

"Ah, so is that why you aren't carrying a restroom pass with you?"

"Mr. Rodriguez, I-"

"Save the excuse, Mr. Venezio. I have a feeling you'll need them for later on in the semester," he suggested before brushing past me.

"Oh, and one more thing Marco," he turned to face me, a cheery smirk on his mouth. "Next time you're in a jam, stop by my office and I'll figure something out," he offered. I gave him a nod after a few seconds, and tightened my backpack straps as I headed off towards my locker. Typically I held my school administrators in high regard, but Mr. Rodriguez evoked a deeper respect from me. It seemed almost commonplace for him to level himself with the crowd. Not very often do you find that in the public school system.

Inside my locker, I was surprised to find an envelop at the bottom. A puzzled expression formed on my face as I picked it up, carefully sliding my finger across the top to slice it open.

"What's that?" a small voice came from behind me.

I turned to see a petite blonde girl, hugging her books to her chest.

"Um, I'm not sure, actually," I had never seen this girl in my life.

"Sorry to intrude, my name's Bethany," she squeaked, "but most people call me Beth," her eyes moving to the floor as she scratched the floor with her shoe.

"Nice to meet you, my name's Marco, but most people call me Marco."

She giggled and looked up into my eyes with an adorable innocence. "Well, Marco, today is my first day and these hallways are a maze. Can you help me find my class?" She asked, shyly.

"Absolutely! What's the room number?"

And just like that, I had made a new friend. But what I didn't see coming, was sure to test my patience and character.

My father, Arsenio Venezio, has his shortcomings as well as his strengths. I've always admired him for his can-do attitude, which was apparent during the years he coached my football and baseball teams. In time, as my teams won more and more games, his level of intensity increased. Sports officials dreaded mediating between him and opposing teams, parents on our sidelines were always more aggressive and supported my dad's coaching style. He soon became the talk of New Mexico after he was tossed out of a state final game for spitting in a referee's face. Although I am grateful for this motivation he instilled in me, I still waver at the impact his business has on our environment. Arsenio Venezio is the CEO of a major oil and gas company, known globally as ViziCo.

My Nike backpack announces my arrival home as I drop it on the kitchen floor, my first instinct leading me to the refrigerator in search of microwave burritos.

"What's up, champ?" My dad asks me as he strolls into the kitchen.

"Eh, same old. Hungry," I state, plainly.

He slaps my back and says, "hey, guess what I picked up earlier today?"

"What's that?"

"Guess."

"Uh… you picked up some clothes from the laundromat?"

"No, smart ass." He spins to pop open the cupboard to produce two tickets.

"What you got there?" I wonder out loud.

"These, my friend, are two tickets to tonight's ball game against the Arizona All-Stars," he explains proudly. "Section J, row 3."

"That's awesome! Row 3?"

"Yep, better get your stuff together here. Leaving in fifteen."

The New Mexican Sun Gods' arena is an extravagant structure, with elaborate statues and jagged edges jutting up at each corner of the complex. Cars were lined up clear down the approaching street, waiting to enter the underground parking garage. My father sped past the line of cars and squealed his tires turning a corner, pulling up to the exclusive entry way for coaches and players.

"Mr. Venezio, good to see ya. Head right in," the ticket master declared.

"So what, these people taking bribes from you?" I joke with him.

This was a big game, The Sun Gods and the All-Stars were neck and neck in the race for the western division title. Tonight's winner would clinch a first round bye in the playoffs.

We took several discreet hallways and a few elevators up to the ViziCo box, overlooking the arena. My dad opened the door and we were greeted with loud welcomings. Lush couches and magnificent paintings made the place feel cozy.

"Jump up over there, I'll swing by in a sec," my dad told me as he made his way over to the bar.

I took a seat in one of the high-swivel chairs on the ledge extending from the box, anxious for tip off. The interior of the structure consisted of a giant floating display, which could maneuver around the arena to provide a more immersive experience. But this one-of-a-kind screen wasn't the only thing that made the Sun God stadium the most unique in the league, it was the notorious 'heat zone', the section of fans located directly behind each basket, the most obnoxious fans in the world. Once upon a time, while an opposing player was lined up for free throws, every person in the 'heat zone' turned around and pulled their pants down to moon the player. He missed both free throws. They still run footage of that on ESPN's not top 10.

My dad found his way to the front of the box, where I sat munching down on some nachos.

"This, is for you," he announced, sliding a tall beer in front of me. He lit a cuban cigar and kicked his feet up on the railing.

"So whaddaya say? Pretty cool, huh?"

"This place is unbelievable!"

"Heh heh, yeah, these guys know how to get the fans involved. You know, your mother would not be happy with me, but everybody's gotta enjoy themselves," he says casually, referring to the beer sitting in front of me.

Just before the half, our best player, Reggie Montgomery, took a shot from half court just as the buzzer went off. The ball hit nothing but net and the place erupted like Mt. Vesuvius. The box was filled with drunks high fiving each other and laughing.

"Marco, I've got a surprise for you. Take a walk with me, would you?" My dad asked me.

We made our way through the turns and twists of the stadium, eventually reaching an elevator.

"You ready for this?" he asks me.

"Ready for what?" I reply.

He punches the button on the elevator and next thing I know, we're walking out onto the court. Sun God players high fived us as we strided into the middle.

"Ladies and gentlemen," the announcer began. "Please welcome, Arsenio and Marco Venezio!"

Fans screamed as I glanced up at the floating display to see myself, looking fresh in my polo.

Booming out in his broadcaster tone, the announcer said "Today Marco will have one chance to win $200,000. All he has to do is jump off a trampoline, over Reggie Montgomery, and dunk from the three point line. Who's ready for some action?"

Anticipation grew from the bleachers like vines on the side of a fence. I caught the basketball with one hand from the referee and took a casual jog to the opposite basket. Electronic sports music blared through the stadium sound system as I stretched my legs.

"On your watch, Marco," the announcer said.

I stretched my neck and gave my dad a determined nod. Then, I took off from the line. I crossed half-court at full speed and leapt aggressively for the trampoline. I bounced violently towards the hoop, my legs completely above the rim. I bent my legs behind me, nearly touching my back as I extended one arm to full length, before slamming the ball down through the net. Everyone's mouths hung open in disbelief. Replays of my three point line dunk reran on the floating display as Reggie and I paraded around the court, one fist outstretched.

"Have you thought about what you're gonna do with all that money?" My dad asked me, clicking his seatbelt and shifting into reverse.

"Mmm, not sure."

"How about saving for college?"

"College? Who needs college when you're a future professional athlete?"

My dad laughed and yanked the wheel as he sped past people waiting in line to exit the complex. People honked at us as several middle fingers extended out of their car windows.

"I'm not going to discourage you, but just be careful. Always nice to have a plan B," he added.

I never really considered college. I was either going straight to the pros, or I would find something else to do with my time. Especially today, with how expensive classes and textbooks are, it's just as wise to find something you're good at that doesn't cost $200,000 dollars.

Chapter Two

"Here, check this one out," Donnie Williams said to his father, sliding a piece of notebook paper with a sketch of Mr. Williams himself.

"Very clever. You could've thrown in a couple more hairs on top, you know," Mr. Williams joked, running his palm over his bald head.

"Look, I've got several meetings to attend to, in addition to dealing with all this press surrounding Helen's affair."

"Helen had an affair?" Donnie asked in a surprised tone.

"You didn't hear? Her and Mr. Vice President himself, someone even got video footage and it's running on CNN," Mr. Williams explained, dragging his briefcase off of the maple wood kitchen table and rustling with his newspaper.

Donnie's face displayed a disgusted expression while he folded his drawing back into his notebook.

"So does that mean you're stepping into her spot?"

"There's a fairly good chance, but don't go around broadcasting that to the whole school. And for God's sake, Donnie, will ya wash your dishes before just tossing them into the dishwasher? I opened it up this morning to find your enchilada all over the place."

Mr. Williams grabbed his blazer off the coat rack and stumbled out the front door, then out to his 2019 Mercedes-Benz.

Later that same day, Donnie, notebook held tight, made the trek down the tall staircase in front of Pioneer's Memorial High School - home to the fightin' Pioneers - located just outside of Washington D.C.

"Wait up, stretch!" Gib called out, hustling downwards after him.

Seconds later, a short, plump, heavy breathing Gib walked up next to Donnie, spitting out words in between breaths.

"Do you," *gasp,* "wanna see," *gasp,* "something crazy?" *gasp.*

"What are you talking about, Gib?"

"Come with me, back to my place. I was searching the internet last night and I found some *wild stuff,* man."

"Whaddaya mean, *wild?"* Donnie looks down at Gib's left hand, a deck of Pokemon cards clenched tightly in his fist.

"Gib, why are you carrying Pokemon cards with you? Didn't you graduate the fifth grade?"

"Eat shit, Donnie. I'm holding these for a friend," Gib shot back.

The two walk past a group of jocks, and one of them cracks up laughing then says, "well if it isn't nerd 1 and nerd 2? You guys should wear matching shirts!"

"Says Mr. I wear ripped jeans for easy access!" says Gib.

The jock takes off after Gib, chasing him around a tree before picking him up and shoving him upside down in a trash can.

Donnie helps Gib out of the trash, brushing some questionable brown substance off of his shoulder.

"Thanks, man. Let's go, I've got mozzarella sticks in my freezer," Gib expressed in a worn-out tone, pulling himself back together.

Gib yanks open the microwave door, revealing a mushy mountain of marvelous mozzarella sticks. He pokes at one of them a couple times before slamming the door shut and cranking the dial. Donnie's slender frame extended out from his sunken position in Gib's beanie bag, controller in hand, playing video games.

"Do you want mayo with your mozzarella sticks?" Gib asked.

"Gib, on what planet do they eat mozzarella sticks with mayonnaise?"

"All the awesome ones," Gib responded in a matter-of-fact tone, jumping onto his bed.

"There's something wrong with you, I just can't figure out what," Donnie concluded.

Gib popped open his laptop and clicked around for a second before saying, "so, are you ready for this?"

"I guess."

"Okay, but before I show you, do you know that chick in our science class, who sits on the right side by Jennifer?"

Donnie scrunched his nose, violently punching buttons on the controller before saying, "huh? Who are you talking about?"

"Y'know, that chick with the blonde hair, sits next to Jennifer in science?"

"Oh, you mean Tara?"

"No, I mean gigglebunny7723," Gib said, turning his laptop around to reveal a highly-suggestive webcam video.

"What!? Hold on, that's her?"

"Sure is! I was surprised too," Gib mused.

"Are you the only one who knows about this?"

"Of course not, she has over 200 daily visitors!" Gib explained.

"No, dip shit. I mean at our school," Donnie fired back.

"Well, as far as I can tell. But don't go around telling people I showed you this."

"Whatever, man. How long have you known?"

"Found her page last week, while I was surfing the good old xxxdoubletake.com."

"Savage."

The next day, Donnie struggled to conceal a boner thinking about Tara in science class.

"Donnie, would you like to provide an illustration of the five layers of soil up on the white board?" His teacher wondered out loud, peering down at him over a pair of reading glasses.

"Um, sure," he replied, stuffing a hand down his pants and readjusting himself in his waistband before slowly raising out of his seat.

"Knock 'em dead, Johnny," Gib joked as Donnie made his way to the front of the classroom.

Donnie offered him a disapproving look as he pried the cap off a red marker.

"This is the organic layer, then the topsoil, the subsoil, after that is the parent material, and finally, the bedrock," Donnie extrapolated, before spinning around quick enough to jar his boner free from his waistband, exposing himself to the entire classroom. Kids laughed as Donnie made an embarrassed glance towards Tara, then fixed himself and sat back down.

"That… was… interesting, Donnie, thank you," his teacher managed to cough up over a smirk.

As soon as Donnie sat down, Gib spun around to give him a double thumbs up.

Donnie was a quiet kid growing up. He liked hot wheels, dinosaurs, and playing video games. But most of all, Donnie loved to draw pictures. He would draw and draw for hours on end, filling entire sketchbooks with animals and cityscapes, cartoon characters and action heros. He became very good at it, and eventually started drawing political cartoons. By fifteen, he drew a cartoon well enough to get published in the school's newspaper. Unfortunately, hardly anyone ever reads those things. His dream was to do weekly political cartoons for the D.C. Tabbernazzle. His father, however, had visions of

Donnie growing into his shoes to become a senator in the HOC.

"My public affairs committee and I have decided at this time, following the recent events in the capitol, it would be best for me to step down as the speaker for the House of Congress," Helen began.

Cameras flashed rapidly as Martha nodded to a gentleman in the front row. "Helen, can you tell us the specifics of your interaction with David Hansel?"

"I'm not in a position to delve into my relationship with David. He has his work, I have my preferences," Helen replied.

Another reporter in the front row catches Helen's eye.

"Helen, was David worth the cost of your position in the house?"

Helen, whose face had turned a shade of red, clears her throat before saying, "although I find your question rather snide, I will say that given the current circumstances within the house, I can look forward to brighter tomorrows. Now, I have time for one more question."

She called on a lady in the third row.

"Is there any available insight in regards to who will be stepping in to fill your role?"

"I'm fairly certain that Jack Williams will be your new speaker in the House of Congress. That's all we have time for, thank you," Helen says before exiting the platform.

Jack, watching the whole time, loosened his tie to relieve the pressure on his neck. The swarm of reporters filed out the front door, buzzing with chatter, as Jack produced a flask to ease the sting of newfound responsibility.

"That's the great thing about high school, man. You show up, watch the girls, skip class and smoke weed," Gib drew to a conclusion, seemingly unaware of the awkward stares he was receiving walking down the hall next to Donnie.

"Yeah, you keep telling yourself that while you're flipping patties at Burger Ace," Donnie joked.

"Mmm, that sounds good right now, you down to skip third and hit the BA?"

"Man, I've got a quiz during third. Why don't you go harass one of your other friends? Oh wait, you don't have any other friends," Donnie mused.

Gib stuck his foot out in an attempt to trip Donnie, which he stepped over before shoving Gib on the shoulder.

"Chill out, bro. Hey, there goes your girlfriend," Gib said after Tara crossed in front of them.

"She's *your* girlfriend, dick munch. I don't watch those webcams."

"Well, maybe you should. Then you wouldn't be so agitated all the time."

"Oh wow, that's such a grown up word, Gib. Would you like a golden star?" Donnie asked sarcastically.

"That hurt, man. That really hurt. I'm gonna skip class and do fun stuff. Good luck with your boring ass quiz."

"I will."

"Fine."
"Fine."
"Out front at 3?"
"Sure."

Chapter Three

As I watch the mountain landscape slide past the interior of my dad's car through the window, with Red Hot Chili Peppers music pouring through the speakers, I suddenly flashback to a time in my younger years, when my mother was still around, she took me downtown to enjoy the annual light parade during Christmas time.

We pull into a parking spot at the entrance to Storm Mountain trailhead. I make my way to the trunk and open it, where I find a bottle of sunscreen and a case of water bottles, in addition to a couple hiker's sticks.

"Map says this trail runs about seven miles in total. We should get back home around two, unless you wanna stop for food on the way back," my dad claims while I slather on sunscreen.

"Whatever works. I drank some pre-workout so good luck keeping up," I say with a smirk.

We lock up the beamer and stride through the gate, glancing up to the monstrous rock awaiting our scale.

As we're maneuvering over the jagged rocks foreshadowing vigorous effort, I ask my dad, "If you could be any animal, which one would it be?"

"Mmm, probably a bird. So I could swoop around and see everything."

The next day brings a new school week. My best friend Joey slaps me on the back as I stand studying a flyer on a bulletin board requesting FoodMates deliverers.

"What's crackin ' Jack?"

"Popcorn and WOOH!" I conclude our signature greeting.

I snatch the flyer off of the bulletin board and we start down the hall towards the third period.

"Class, repeat after me. Necesito beber agua."

"Necesito beber agua," everyone declared.

"Necesito usar la computadora."

"Necesito usar la computadora."

"Good, now, yes, Joey?" Mrs. Estrella answered.

Joey lowered his hand and said, "Necesito salir la escuela."

Mrs. Estrella laughed and said, "Very good, Joey, but you may not leave school unless there's a good enough reason."

"I have sex therapy." The whole class busted out in giggles.

"Inappropriate, Joey. No more smart-alec remarks."

The bell sounded, signaling the beginning of lunch.

"Alright, now don't forget to turn in this week's grammar practice on your way out!"

Kids filed out the doorway, while I stayed behind to ask a question.

"Um, Mrs. Estrella?"

"Yes, Marco?"

"Well, I know this may be of inconvenience, but I was wondering, is there any time after school when you could help me go over some of the homework?"

Mrs. Estrella lets out a long sigh, clears her glasses with her shirt, places them back on her nose, and says, "I suppose, Marco. How about this. If you meet me in the back parking lot at 3:30, I can take you to my house for a personal vocabulary session. Sound good?"

"Sounds great, Mrs. Estrella. See you then!"

I find my way into the cafeteria, grab a lunch tray, and park across the table from Joey.

"What up, Sharky Marky?"

"Don't ever call me that."

Joey laughs and says, "ease up, man. You've got options around here."

Between chomps of PB&J, I spurt out, "what the hell are you talking about?"

"You see those girls over there? They're obviously talking about you."

"Where?"

Joey points across the lunchroom to a group of gothic overweight girls, melancholy as molasses.

"No, not them, over there."

At the adjacent table, Bethany, Natalie, and several other girls catch my glance and look down, giggling.

"They want the D, brodog."

"I guess I'll have to find out."

There's a pause between us.

Then, out of nowhere, Joey says, "Bro, my advertisement tech class is doing sample commercials, and I got this wicked idea for a water bottle company!"

"Alright, let's hear it."

"Okay, so, these kids are hanging out on a blacktop. Each of them has a different bottle. And one of them says, yo man, what can your water bottle do? So one of them flips his bottle, and it lands perfectly. And everybody goes woah! And the next kid, he shoots his water bottle like a basketball, and drains it in the net, and they go woah! And the third kid, he takes out one of my Rocky Mountain water bottles, and walks over to this guy with really bad skin cancer. And he pours it over this guys head, and the skin cancer just melts off this guys face. And everyone goes WOAH! And the narrator cuts in just as my logo appears on screen, and says, Rocky Mountain water, filtered over 7,000 times."

There's a moment of silence in between us. Then Joey says, "so what do you think? Pretty tight huh?"

"I don't know, man. I'm not some marketing aficionado. I think you need a freaking girlfriend, Joey."

"Yeah, I'm gonna science the shit outta this whole life thing."

Later on, I'm one of the few students left who are exiting the school, and once again, I run into Mr. Rodriguez.

"Mr. Venezio, pleasure to see you again."

"Roddy G, what's happenin?"

"Please refrain from calling me that, Mr. Venezio."

I give out a slight chuckle before he stops me cold in my tracks, and says, "and I hope you intend on staying out of trouble, off of school grounds as well as inside them."

I look up at him with a bit of surprise spreading over my face, then I manage to spit out "ab- absolutely, Mr. R."

"Very well. Now, carry on."

I brushed off my shoulders as I left the building, wondering what that was all about.

Mrs. Estrella leaned against her beat up VW, her large circular sunglasses flashing rays of sun, giving the appearance of stars in her eyes.

"Marco, you're ten minutes late."

"Sorry, I got caught up with Mr. Rodriguez in the hallway."

"Ah, I see. Well, we better get going. Hop in."

Mrs. Estrella burns rubber turning the corner into her neighborhood, and skids to a halt in front of her house. My backpack empties its contents from the backseat, spewing binders and paper across the dash.

"Oops, sorry kiddo."

I let out a feeble laugh and said, "jeez, Mrs. Estrella. You've been watching too many action films."

Inside, her walls are lined with abstract Mexican canvases and articulate affirmations of family oriented happiness.

"We can set up shop at the kitchen table, if you wanna grab a seat there."

I give a sigh of relief as I plop down, releasing my baggage.

"Would you like some lemonade? I have a pitcher full in the fridge," Mrs. E offered.

"That'd be sweet."

As she poured a couple glasses, I studied her enticing curves giving shape to a sophisticated grey dress.

She walked over and placed a glass in front of me. I picked it up and drained the entire thing with three giant gulps.

"Wow, Marco. You'd think I found you in the desert."

"Something like that. Can I get another?"

"Go right ahead. Plenty more where that came from."

Succulent slices of lemon complimented the residue dripping down the sides of the glass, as well as on my forehead during my attempt to conceal my growing erection.

I looked up to find Mrs. Estrella eyeing my pants, and she said, "Marco, you know, puberty is a very natural thing."

I swallowed hard as I tried to come up with something. Anything. Come on, Marco.

"In fact, I think it can be academically beneficial if you allow for occasional release."

She reached slowly for my jeans, grabbing the bulge protruding from my slender frame. I gasped at the sensation of her grip, the sight of her red polished fingernails exploring my line. She was beginning to unzip my jeans, right as her husband appeared at the top of the stairs.

"Honey, is this tie too flashy?" He asked, fiddling with the fabric long enough to give us time to rearrange ourselves.

"Not flashy enough, dear." She answered him cheerfully.

So I walk into this 7-11 convenience store, a couple cans of vegetables waiting for my personal dinner party. I give the cashier a nod and walk over to the nacho bar, where I grabbed a handful of hot sauce packets and stuffed them in my pocket. As I'm walking out, the cashier makes a big deal out of it. Cussing and ranting over a couple packets of sauce. I just kept saying "siete. Siete."

He followed me out the door and threatened to call the police if I came back. I yelled "what!? Didn't catch that!"

I swagger over to my busted up bicycle with the back tire blown out, which I had been riding around on the bare rim. Just then, the bus pulls up and I drop my bag, spilling stuff all over the sidewalk. I holler out a couple profanities, pull my stuff together, and proceed to yank the bike up onto the rack.

I plop down inside the bus. The bus lurches forward until the driver slams on the brakes and says, "hey man. Hey, man. Man!"

I look up at the rearview and he says, "you forgot the wheel bar."

So I stand up and spin around to see an old geezer cracking up, sipping on a fast food cup. I say, "what are you looking at, geezer?"

I stomp towards the front of the bus and mumble to myself, "I'll smash that damn cup in your face."

I adjust the wheel bar accordingly, and get back on the bus.

Later down the road, I grab my gear and head for the bike shop. Once I managed to get inside with all my stuff, the guys took my bike and set it on the rack for examination. A few minutes later, they came out and let me know that since I had been riding around on the rim, that I would have to buy a bike tube, tire, AND rim, the total running close to $115 dollars. At this point, I had spent all day panhandling and was not in the mood to sit around and play that game again.

My bike is a classic. It's an Edoardo Bianchi Cortina, from Milano, Italy. I bought it for $350. It came with a bike rack, cup holder, and 24 gears. The thing gets going. But, I'll have to pull together some more cash before I can get this FoodMates business rolling. No pun intended. Or maybe I did.

Anyways, I managed to jack a spare tire from an abandoned bike and fix the ole' cruiser. I set the whole thing up on my phone, and got going pretty quick. Keep in mind, this is the first job I've ever had.

My first gig was a delivery 45 minutes away, and when I got there, the guy met me out front and said, "hey, man, good to see ya. Give me a sec, I just gotta run inside and grab my wallet."

I said, "that works."

5 minutes passed. Nothing.

10 minutes. I tried calling him on my phone, but he didn't answer. This damn guy was gonna pay me for this double sausage pepperoni pizza with extra cheese and sliced pickles or I was gonna stuff it in his mailbox. Luckily, his wife pulled up a few minutes later, and I explained the situation to her in my calmest tone possible. She went inside to find out what the deal was.

Turns out, the dude hopped in the shower (really? wow) and forgot all about his food. She paid me and tipped 30%.

On my second gig, I was given precise instructions to hop the fence into the backyard, let myself into the sliding glass door, and my payment would be waiting next to the couch. Interesting. Once I pulled up, I hopped the fence and a ferocious dog with slobber longer than Niagra Falls approached me at an alarming rate of speed. I struggled with the back gate, but couldn't get it open. Before the dog could reach me, I took out the taco eleven pack and let it fly. That kept the dog busy while I jumped back over. Freakin' pricks.

My third gig was a game changer. I was given directions to an old trailer park on the outskirts of town. I visited the 70's Shack, where the cashier informed me that this guy was a regular and usually tipped pretty well. I strapped up my bike with his four veggie sub sandwiches and headed out.

Upon arrival, I noticed a hippie flag and green party political signs scattered across the front lawn. I rang the doorbell twice, and an older guy appeared with John Lennon sunglasses and a jean jacket with a backwards pub hat.

"Groovy, man. Step right in."

"Uh, okay."

The inside was covered with tapestries and lava lamps. Several jars of weed sat on a vintage coffee table next to graphic magazines.

"Sit down, man." He motioned over to a giant purple bean bag.

"Here, take a hit of this stuff, man."

"Nah, I'm good. Hey, did you wanna pay for this food or what?"

"Calm, brother. Meditation is a virtue." He lit a joint and sat back in his chair. Reggae music drifted through wooden speakers placed variantly throughout the living room.

"What do they call you, man?"

"Marco. Marco Venezio."

"Far out, man."

"I guess. What's your name?"

"Coyote Bongwater."

Chapter Four

Graphite strokes Donnie's paper slightly as he adds shadowing to his newest masterpiece, while he lounges in front of the television, shoveling cheesy tortilla chips into his gaping mouth. He makes a few final revisions and flips his pencil onto the table, kicking his feet up next to it and leaning back. The cartoon displays a race car driver in a broken down car, steam rising under a popped hood. Next to the car stands a giant Plesiosaurus, grazing on a tree. The driver is asking, "Hey, you have any idea when that meteor is supposed to hit?"

Donnie is pleased with his creation. He takes a swig of grape juice, and lets out a satisfied sigh. On the television screen flashes a commercial invitation to send in cartoons to the D.C. Tabbernazzle for a cash reward of $500 dollars. Donnie nearly pisses himself as he jumps out of his chair in excitement.

"That's enough to put a down payment on a car!" He declares. He hardly sleeps that night, giddy with anticipation for the world to behold his piece.

The next day, two blueberry waffles explode violently out of the toaster and onto a plate, which Donnie snatches off of the counter on his way out the door. He slides his stamped cartoon into the mail and slaps his skateboard down on the sidewalk, his backpack hanging off one shoulder as he glides away.

It's a typical Friday at Pioneer's Memorial High. Classes are noisy with inattentive hooligans, itching for the bell to ring so they can begin their weekend shenanigans. During his final period, Donnie scribbles drawings in his notebook, then proceeds to fall asleep on top of his desk, a pool of saliva collecting around his face. He wakes up to an empty classroom with Tara poking him with a pencil.

"Wake up, silly head!" She squeaks in an adorable voice.

Donnie jerks up from his desk and says, "what? I'm good. Tara? What are you still doing here?"

"I saw you passed out and wanted to check if you were okay. And, wanted to give you this." She reaches in her pocket and pulls out a small piece of paper, then hands it to Donnie.

202-756-4298 xoxo, Tara

"Text me after school, we should hangout. My place?" She giggles and scurries out of the classroom.

Donnie hustles home, eager to see what this night has in store for him. This is the first time that a girl has invited him to her place. Donnie walks inside and heads straight for the bathroom. He pulls out his haircut kit from under the sink, cranks dirty rap music on his bluetooth speaker, and begins shaving at his scalp.

He sends Tara a message - 'Hey, It's Donnie. What time you wanna meet up?'

He gets in the shower and takes a good 45 minutes, not thinking about what could happen at all. Then, he wonders to himself, should I be considering possible situations? What do expert players think about before hanging out with a girl whom they wanna get with? Do they think at all? What if something awkward happens? What if I go in for the kiss right when she opens the door? What if she wants to have a nice sit down meal over candle light? What if her mother is home? What if she never texts back? And do I have a condom? He believes with 50 percent certainty that he has a pack of condoms under a pile of his old kid stuff inside one of his bedroom drawers.

He gets out of the shower, dries off, and checks his phone. One message- from Tara.

'Hey sleepyhead =P XD 8 pm, 143 Stansberry Lane'

Yes.

A young, crisp Donnie steps off the bus with at least half a can of body spray dispersed over his clothes. He strolls up to her door, and knocks three times. Hmm. No cars in the driveway, Donnie notices. Her parents must be gone. An old, army looking man yanks open the door with a mean glare in his eyes.

"Who the hell are you?"

"I- I was looking for Tara?"

"Who?"

"Is this 143?"

"No, jackass. Now get the hell off my porch before I show you my gun collection!"

Donnie turns and beats cheeks out of there. Halfway down the street, he manages to catch his breath, and then realizes he went one street too far.

He finds the correct house, and sends her a text. A few minutes later, she's out front dressed in skin tight yoga pants with a spaghetti strap top and slippers, her hair braided.

"Come inside quick! Before my parents see you!"

They rush down to the basement where her room is.

"Sit here, I'm gonna pick a movie to watch. And don't be too loud."

"Right. Okay."

Donnie pulls out his phone and scrolls through Instagram. A picture of Gib pops up, it's a mirror selfie with him holding up a vacuum. Caption - life suxx (puking emoji, broken heart emoji).

Donnie likes the picture and says to himself, "sorry Gibby." Then comments, 'clean up your attitude'.

A few moments later, and Tara is downstairs, this time with no pants on and a couple movies in her hand.

"Do you wanna watch 'Return of the Poon Slayer 3' or 'My Life as a Nincompoop'?"

"Uh, the first one?"

"I thought so."

She pops in the disc and jumps onto the couch.

"Dang it. I forgot the remote. Donnie?"

"What? You expect me to get it?"

She looks at him and curls her bottom lip and makes sad puppy dog eyes.

"Fine, but if I get up to get the remote, you owe me."

The GHX logo appears on screen, with the accompanying epic sound effect. Tara pulls the blanket off of her bed and spreads it over her and Donnie.

"No phones during the movie."

"Whatever. What is this anyway, Egyptian Cotton?"

Tara scrunches her face and says, "I have no idea, Donnie. Does it matter?"

"Guess not. Just trying to make conversation."

"Uh huh. Why don't you scooch a little closer?" Tara pats the spot next to her on the couch.

Donnie smiles and slides over close enough so that he feels her warm, tender legs against his basketball shorts. The opening scene begins with a guy, maybe 18, dragging himself down a long desert highway. Out of nowhere, a party bus with girls in bikinis pulls up next to him

"Hey stranger, need a lift?" One of the girls calls out.

The man gazes up into the sun, then raises a hand to block it. At first, he wonders if he is hallucinating. Then, he looks down at his pants and notices a bulge growing slowly.

"Looks like I've already got one."

The girls all giggle. One of them says, "get on. We can take care of that."

Donnie and Tara both let out a nervous laugh. The next scene begins with the desert guy drowning in girls, heavy kissing taking place. Donnie places a hand on Tara's leg, then gives her a slight, gentle rub, feeling the cozy texture of her underwear. Tara looks over at Donnie with lust in her eyes, and then rearranges his hand over her vagina. She lets out a soft moan, as Donnie applies pressure to her sensitive zone. He leans over, and plants a gentle kiss on her neck. They find each other's mouths, and begin making out passionately. The kissing gets more intense, and Tara maneuvers her hand into Donnie's pants, squeezing his dick with fervor. Donnie moans and begins pulling her shirt up her back and over her head. She wore no bra under her shirt, revealing two perfectly round breasts. Donnie squeezes one and sucks on the other, while Tara works on his pants. They continue heavy touching and wrestle each other onto her bed.

Fifteen minutes later, the two lay in a heap of clothes and bed sheets, breathing heavily.

"You wanna do that again?" Donnie asks.

"If you want to."

Donnie and Tara go at it for another three hours, before she forces him to sneak out the basement window for fear of waking her parents. Donnie skateboards home, a crisp evening air complementing his newfound manhood.

He woke up the next day to some cereal and Saturday morning cartoons. After slurping down the milk, he went straight out to the mailbox box to find a utility bill and a letter from the D.C. Tabbernazzle. He went inside, tossed the utility bill on the counter, and sliced open the letter from the paper.

"This better be good," he said to himself.

'Dear Mr. Williams,

We are very excited to inform you that your cartoon will be featured in next weekend's edition of the D.C. Tabbernazzle! Yours is the first cartoon printed in our paper by somebody under 25. Included in this envelope is a check for $500, your cash prize for winning our contest. Keep up the good work, Donnie.

Sincerely,
D.C. Tabbernazzle Comics Editor

"Sick! Hey dad! Dad!" Hmm. Must be at work. Donnie rushes to get dressed and skateboards down to the bank to cash his check, then over to the used car dealership.

"All these cars require 500 down. Good credit, no credit, doesn't matter. All you do is sign the X and she's yours," the dealer explained.

"Sweet. What about this one?"

"Oh, that thing? You drive anything else off this lot and you'll be wishing you had a V8," the dealer jokes.

A smile grows on Donnie's face.

Donnie took his Cadillac CTS-V up to a moderate sized hill overlooking the city that very night. With rap music playing, Donnie rolled a joint and lit it, taking a drag and studying the lights off in the distance. What a time, he thought. What a time. After a few more drags, he experienced a rush of euphoria as the marijuana ran through his veins like it was carrying a baton. He turned the music up louder and opened the door, letting smoke float up up and away. He sent Gib a snapchat of him, puffing on his doob, his interior illuminated by the cabin light and his head bobbing to the music. Gib sent one back that said, 'WTF!?? Drive your ass over here now! We're partying'.

Donnie pulls up in a joyful daze, his previous trip a blur at best. He shifts up and turns the key backwards, then pauses a second, a confused look on his face. He cracks the door open and slowly opens it with his leg, then stumbles out of the car amongst a cloud of kush announcing his arrival. He mosies around to the passenger side, where he reexamined his piss poor parking job. He starts cracking up laughing, and gets back in the car. With his door hanging open, he pulls away from the curb, and tries again. He gets out and checks again. This time, he's clear up in the middle of the sidewalk. His door still open, he pulls away for round three. By now, his face is displaying a stupefied expression. He gets out to check again, this time, he's a solid eight feet from the curb.

"Ah, hell."

He gives it another go. Painfully slow, he directs the steering wheel as he inches towards the sidewalk. Steady, and, there! He jumps out to clarify the validity of his efforts. Fuckin good enough, he thinks to himself. He sits back in the car, and gathers his phone and wallet. He pulls on his keys, but they won't come out. What in the hell? He searches his dash for a sign. Some clue as to why on Earth his damn keys won't come out of the ignition. He pulls and pulls. Finally, he texts Gib.

'Yo, I can't get my keys out the ignition. Come help'.

Gib texts back, 'are you freaking kidding me?'

Gib walks out onto the street in boxer shorts, wearing his mother's dress shoes.

"Are you really this dumb?"

"Dude, I don't know what's going on. I can't figure it out."

"Get out, dipshit. Let me try."

Gib jumps in the driver's seat and pulls on the keys.

"I already tried that, asshole," Donnie declares.

Gib searches the cabin for a clue. Five minutes go by. Nothing.

"Bro, what the fuck did you do to your car?"

"Fuck if I know."

The two of them look around the car for another few minutes, completely dumbfounded. Suddenly, Gib looks down, and shifts the car from neutral into park. Then, he pulls the keys straight out. He looks Donnie in the face, and says, "here you go, dumbass."

"Wait how'd you do that?" Donnie asks, surprised.

"You forgot to shift into park."

"God damn it."

The next day at school, Gib and Donnie are working together on an experiment in chemistry class.

"Bro, I'm telling you, she literally snuck me into her basement, flipped on a movie, and just started sucking on my dong," Donnie reiterated.

"I still don't believe you." Gib takes a dropper from the pan and carefully measures off three drops of chemical X into beaker 1. He pours an additional 50 grams of sodium and mixes it together.

"We need chemical Y from the front, be a dear and grab that, would you?"

Donnie shoots him a dirty look, shakes his head, and walks off.

While Donnie is looking for the final ingredient, Gib whips out his phone and checks Tara, or rather, gigglebunny7723's webcam page. What Gib finds, leaves his mouth hanging wide open.

Donnie comes back, measures the appropriate amount of chemical Y, and is just about to add it in when Gib stops him.

"Dude, is that you?"

Gib shows him a video that Tara posted, of her sneaking into her own room and sucking a mystery man on the bed.

"Bro, those are definitely your Adidas on the bed."

Donnie, who is too stunned to realize what he is doing, pours the entire container of chemical Y into the beaker, causing a mini explosion in the middle of the classroom.

Chapter Five

"Coyote Bongwater? What kind of name is that?" I asked the man smoking weed in his retro trailer.

"It's a name I earned back in the seventies. Me and my buddies had a groovy little smoke spot where we would pass this bong around in a circle. One night, one of my pals dared me to drink the water out of the bong. So I did. Finished every last drop."

I scanned him with a concerned expression.

"And after I did, I howled at the moon like a Coyote. Man, those were the days."

"I don't know what to say, except that your food is getting cold," I cut back in.

"Oh, right. Here's your cash."

"No tip?"

Coyote Bongwater gave me a look, and said, "I already offered you my weed. It's good stuff, too. Grew it myself."

"You grow your own weed?"

"Of course! Got myself a whole field! Over a hundred plants!" Coyote Bongwater exclaimed.

"And if you were smart, you'd ask me if you could trim my bushes for money," he hinted.

"Nah, that ain't me."

"What a shame. See what people need to do, is take back control. We need to fight the system with our own produce, man. Grow our own food, weed, generate our own electricity. Pretty soon, when everything caves in on us, the people who rely on the system will bite the dust," Coyote Bongwater scoffed. "And I hear they've got something big in the works. The boys in the capitol. Some type of massive power plant, capable of powering two United States. But twice the power means twice the pollution. You keep that thing running long enough and our ozone turns into beef stew."

I paused a second to consider his previous statement.

"You know, I guess you're right. So how do we stop it?"

"Boycott. We yank the rug out from under these guys. Then we kick em while they're down," Coyote said in a violent tone.

"Why don't we just elect someone who prioritizes environmental policy reform?" I suggest.

"That's too mainstream, man."

I laughed and said, "alright, man. Well you have a good rest of your night," and start for the front door.

"Wait, man. You sure you don't want a joint for the road?"

"I'm okay. Thanks anyways."

I closed the door behind me, Coyote took another drag and said, "what a stiffler, man."

A few days later, I was working the combo on my locker when Joey approached me.

"Mark the fart, what's good?"

"What the hell did you just call me?"

"Nevermind. Hey, if you're not busy on Friday, we should hit that bowling alley on Cadoa. Seems pretty lit," Joey suggested.

"The one on Cadoa? Really?"

"Yeah, they've got unlimited soda during happy hour."

"I'll think about it," I replied.

"You can even invite Natalie and Bethany. You know, do a double date."

"Joey, you can't handle yourself around girls," I joked.

"The hell I can't!"

I laughed and slammed my locker shut. "We'll see. I've got priorities."

"Visiting xxxdoubletake doesn't count as a priority," Joey scoffed.

I shook my head and played that one off.

"Class, repeat after me. Yo escribo un libro nuevo."

"Yo escribo un libro nuevo," we repeated.

"Mrs. Estrella?"

"Yes, Jaxon?"

"Dónde están las drogas?"

"Go out in the hall, Jaxon."

The bell rang, and students began exiting the classroom.

"Don't forget the homework! Three page essay on Don Quixote, due next Wednesday! And Marco, please stay for a second. I need to have a word with you."

Confused, I slowly made my way to the front of the room. She waited until everybody had left, and began with, "Mr. Venezio. We have unfinished business," before extending her hand, waving me closer with her pointer finger.

"Umm, I-"

"Shhh, don't talk, Marco. You're a mystery and I'm gonna get to the bottom of this case," she said seductively before eyeing my lower body.

Mrs. Estrella, I-"

Just then, Mr. Rodriguez busted through the door.

"Mrs. Estrella, your company is requested in the teacher's lounge."

She looked up at him, a disapproving expression growing over her face.

"Now! You're not being paid to fan the breeze."

He straightened his tie and marched out of the classroom.

Mrs. Estrella stood from her chair, and said, "we'll revisit this another day," then winked at me.

I mean, it's not like I don't think Mrs. Estrella is hot. She definitely is.

But, if Mr. Rodriguez, or somebody else caught me doing stuff with her, especially at school, who knows what would happen. She would probably be fired. I would almost certainly be suspended. And all the kids would find out. But what if that's a good thing? I would be remembered forever as a legend. Eh, I think I'll take my chances with Natalie and Bethany first. Maybe Mrs. Estrella can give me some relationship advice.

Coincidentally, it was that same day that I turned a corner in the hallway and nearly bumped into Natalie and Bethany.

"Hey, what's up?" I asked.

"Nothin, what's up with you?" Bethany asked me.

"Y'know, same old. Hey, I was meaning to ask you girls. I was thinking about driving to Desert Flags this weekend, wanna come?"

"That sounds fun! Natalie, are you busy this weekend?" Beth asked her.

"Not really. Would it be just us three?"

I hesitated, and thought about Joey. A voice in my head said, 'don't bring Joey. He's a hazard! He'll block any chance to get it in with these girls!' Another voice in my head said, 'come on, bro! Joey's cool enough! He'll smooth over relations! Maybe even attract more girls or something!' 'Yeah, but he'll want to get like four funnel cakes and start shit with the employees and get you kicked out.' 'Oh now you're just being an asshole.'

"Hello? Marco?" Natalie said.

"Sorry, uh, I was gonna bring Joey. That cool with you guys?"

"Who's Joey?"

"He's a friend. Don't worry, he's pretty chill," I answered.

They looked at eachother, shrugged their shoulders, and said, "ok. That works."

"Alright, awesome. Pick you up on Saturday in the school parking lot. 10 A.M."

So Friday night, Joey calls me while I'm playing video games.

"Sup?"

"Sup."

"You still down to hit the bowling alley? I can swing by in my mom's car."

"Nah."

"What do you mean, nah?" Joey asks, frustrated by my sudden change of heart.

"Well, I saw Bethany and Natalie in the hallway, and thought, why not invite them to Desert Flags on Saturday? So that's the plan."

"What the hell, man?"

"You can come too. If you promise not to be a jackass," I offered him.

"You act like you're not the jackass here," Joey fires back.

"Do you wanna go with us or not?"

"What time? I've gotta watch Saturday cartoons or I'll be in a bad mood all weekend."

"You would. 10 A.M. School parking lot."

"Word."

Later on, I walk downstairs and my dad's watching basketball on the TV.

"Dad, can I borrow the car tomorrow?"

"For what?" He responds, his eyes still fixated on the screen.

"Me and some friends wanna-"

"Oh! Man! That's brutal!" My dad yells at the TV.

"What? What Happened?"

"Reggie Montgomery just socked a guy in the teeth! Damn that's gotta hurt!" He bellowed out before stuffing his mouth full of caramel popcorn.

"Wow. Anyways, me and my friends wanna-"

"Look at em go! He's punching the referee now!"

Players clear the benches and a brawl starts on court.

"That's gonna be on ESPN later!"

I laugh in subtle agreement.

"I'll leave the keys on the counter."

"Cool, thanks dad."

I show up at the school parking lot, and the first thing Joey says when he gets in the car is, "here, take a swig of this stuff."

"Joey, what is that?" I asked in a concerned tone, looking at a bottle inside a brown paper bag.

"Don't ask, don't tell."

"Oh, that's reassuring."

"Come on, Marky Yarky, a little pre-game never hurt," Joey fooled.

"Yarky? That's not even a word, idiot."

"Suit yourself. I'm gonna down this whole bottle with a pack of motion sickness pills."

"You're gonna shit blood," I asserted.

10 minutes passed. No sign of the girls.

"I thought you invited girls, Mark. What the F," Joey said, growing impatient.

"Calm down. They'll be here."

15 minutes flew by. Then, we noticed two gorgeous babes walking towards us dressed in bikinis.

"Woah."

"Woah is right, mi amigo. Told you they'd come," I reminded him.

They opened the back doors and jumped in the beamer.

"Sorry we're late. Bethany had to find her swimsuit. Dumb slut," Natalie joked.

"Shut up, bitch! Perfection takes time," Bethany replied.

"No worries, ladies. Here, have a drink of this," Joey said, handing back the mystery bottle.

"We're good," Bethany said.

"Gimme that," Natalie demanded, ripping the bottle out of Joey's hand.

"So fiesty," I commented from the driver's seat.

"Let's get this party bus moving, slick. There's probably a line at this place," Joey guessed.

"Yeah, yeah. Where's the tunes, Joey? Play some damn music," I said before peeling out of the school parking lot.

Later down the road, I'm driving down the highway with the sunroof open and music blasting, feeling like a million bucks. Natalie had taken a few more swigs out of Joey's bottle, and was pretty drunk. I shit you not, while on the highway going 70+, this chick climbed from the backseat and stood out of the sunroof on my dad's beamer. Joey had to pull her back down before she got hit with a rock or swallowed a bug.

We showed up to Desert Flags ready to tear the place up. It was something in the air that day. I could taste mischief on my tongue, the dazzling New Mexican Sun beating down on our heads. The line to get in was ridiculous, so we snuck around to the side and hopped the fence. That saved us 45 dollars each. Once inside, we went straight for the giant wave pool with the Dr. Fizzle logo printed on the bottom. We found a spot to leave our towels, and approached the ominous tidal zone. As we were getting deeper into the water, there was a kid floating on an inflatable donut that got flipped completely off his tube. Everybody saw from across the pool, it was hilarious. In the peak tidal zone, waves reached over 20 feet high. Small children weren't allowed past the play zone. After splashing each other and goofing around for about 15 minutes, we got out and dried off in the blazing hot sunlight.

As we were all sprawled out on our beach chairs, Joey looked over at me and said, "dime piece, 9 o'clock."

I glance over to my left to see a gorgeous babe with buttcheecks hanging out of her bathing suit.

"We might have to confiscate her v-card, Joey."

We started cracking up, the girls gave us dirty looks and scoffed at us.

"You guys are real mature, you know that?" Bethany asked rhetorically.

"Hey, we know how to appreciate a sexy girl when we see one," Joey answered.

"Whatever, we're going to get snow cones."

"Ooh, grab me a purple one, with vanilla syrup," Joey requested.

"Get it yourself, dweeb," Bethany said before they got up from their chairs and walked away.

"Oh man, we're gonna get so much ass at this place."

"Shut up, Joey."

Afterwards, we decided to start out slow with a ride on the gigantic ferris wheel. Us 4 boarded the swinging cart, and upwards we went. The girls started snapchatting with their phones, and Joey stuffed napkins in his mouth and started throwing spit wads off the side.

"Savage, bro! See if you can hit the operator!"

Joey produced another wad of paper and saliva from his mouth, and cut in with his sports announcer voice.

"We got a 3-2 count. Joey's been lights out all day, let's see if he brings that nasty curve. He winds, kicks high, and-" Joey hurled the spitwad off the ferris wheel all the way from the top.

We could see the small white ball carry in the breeze before SPLAT! Right on top of the operator's head. Laughter and high fives went around in our cart. A prime beginning to our day.

Following our ferris wheel ride, we made our way over to the large, rotating swing ride. After waiting in line for a few minutes, we were strapping into the chairs. The ride started up, and soon we were gliding through the air at a moderate speed. Joey sat next to me, flying through the air a good 10 feet away since all the chairs were separated. The girls sat a few rows ahead of us, unaware of the trouble we were about to cause. Joey shouted over at me during the middle of the ride.

"Yo Marky! Check this out!"

He slipped his heel out from the back of his right shoe and flung it straight into the air. I watched that thing sail for a good 50 yards before landing in some poor guys nachos. The concomitant was of course, one unhappy nacho connoisseur. You couldn't duplicate those two shots in a million years. The ride operator had no freakin' idea. Everybody knows shoeless Joe, and now they know one shoe Joe.

We got lucky and found four speedpasses in the trash, so from that point on we waltzed straight to the front of the line, no sweat. Next, we came across the Tower of Zoom, the tallest ride at Desert Flags.

"Uh uh, I am not getting on that thing," Natalie declined.

"Why not? It's 100 percent safe," Joey said.

"Don't make me ride it alone, girl. You're coming with!" Bethany told her.

"Ugh, fine."

We locked ourselves in, and frightening music started playing on the sound system. A man's voice began, saying, "captain! The overhaul drive has blown past the limit! We're approaching light speed!"

"There's nothing we can do now. Brace yourself for time travel."

Then, a loud laser noise exploded through the speakers as we shot directly upwards along the tower. Up and down, up and down, several times. After the third time, Natalie leaned over and sprayed vomit all over the people watching below, causing several other people to throw up too. Joey wouldn't stop screaming, and for a moment I got really lightheaded and thought I was gonna pass out. Bethany was the only one who seemed like she was enjoying the Tower of Zoom. At the end, we unbuckled ourselves and staggered out of the exit, with people cursing profanities at us. The Tower of Zoom became the Tower of Gloom.

The girls needed to find the restroom to get Natalie cleaned up. Joey and I were starving, so we paid a visit to Armando's World Infamous Burrito Shack, est. 2007. We ordered two smothered burritos, and they were so big that they hung over the sides of the plate. Joey, being the sloppy animal he is, bought 5 churros as well. We found a spot on an empty bench and sat to eat.

"Hold on, I'll be right back," Joey said. 2 minutes later, he came back with a stack of napkins and a bottle of ghost pepper sauce.

"Don't tell me. You're upgrading to flaming hot spit wads?"

Joey, laughing and shaking his head, took the cap off the bottle and poured out at least half of its contents over his burrito.

"Gotta do what you gotta do."

We practically inhaled our smothered burritos, and then sat back to digest and people watch. One little girl, walking with her parents, dropped her ice cream cone and started bawling her eyes out. Right then, a clown walking on stilts folded over to hand her a new one.

A few minutes later, the girls arrived from their trip to the restroom.

"Took ya long enough," Joey snarled.

"Shut up, Joey. This was all your fault!" Bethany asserted.

"MY fault!? How is this my fault?"

"You shouldn't have given her any alcohol in the car."

"No, it's fine, Beth. We're okay now," Natalie expressed herself.

"Alright, great. So you'll come with us on more rides?" I asked her.

"No, me and Natalie are gonna hang out by the pool. Meet you there after?"

"Whatever you guys wanna do. The park closes in three hours, so we'll meet you there some time before then."

Joey and I hopped from one ride to another, zooming past the crowds with our scavenged speedpasses. Giant winding roller coasters, a magnificent swinging sailboat, viciously spinning tea cups, you name it. After awhile, we took a break from the electric rides and took a hike up to the top of the monstrous genie-themed slide. We each got a piece of 'magic' carpet, rubbed the 'magic' lamp, and took off down the slide. Midcourse, Joey rolled over and switched lanes, knocking me into the other lane as well.

"Joey, you dick!"

He couldn't stop laughing.

Once we reached the bottom, I chased Joey through the crowd, trying to punch him.

After we had settled down, I looked down at my watch.

"Alright, we got time for one more ride before we have to get the girls."

"Ooh, lets ride the mind-bender again!" Joey suggested.

"Why don't we try something different?"

"Hmm, oh, I know, let's ride the slingshot!"

"That costs money, Joey. I didn't bring enough cash."

"Damnit. Umm, well what about that one?"

"Joey, I'm not getting on that thing."

"Why not?"

"Joey, knock it off. We're not doing it."

"What? Are you, *chicken?* Bawk bawk bawk! Chicken alert!"

"Screw you, man."

"Aw, poor little baby. Do you need a sippy cup?"

"Ugh, FINE! I'll ride it with you! But promise you won't pull any more stunts."

"That's more like it."

It looked colossal from across the park, but once we walked up to face the enormous Interstellar Express, I thought I was looking at an elevator to the moon. Videos played on TV screens showing people's faces as they experienced the 117 mph acceleration down the track, then straight up for what seemed like a mile into the sky.

Signs displayed warnings of possible injury and death. People exiting the ride stumbled away, crying and readjusting their clothes.

I overheard one guy in line say, "I heard one guy hit a bug on the top and got a bruise the size of a watermelon."

"You sure about this?"

"Mark, don't ditch on me now. This is the fastest and tallest roller coaster in America. If we ride this, we're gonna get so much ass."

So I reluctantly sat down on the alien-themed leather seat, and pulled the safe-guard over me. Joey locked himself in place, and began making animal noises and shaking his fists and head rambunctiously. Small children watched him with concerned expressions.

A voice on the intercom said, "thank you for choosing the Interstellar Express. Your number one choice for cross-dimensional travel. We encourage you to keep your seatbelt fastened at all times, and avoid extending any limbs from the rocket ship. Safe travels!" Then, the rocket blast sounded and we sped away from the platform. I thought my face was melting. I couldn't see anything. It seemed like we just kept going faster and faster. Then, we reached the end of the acceleration zone and the rocket ship curved straight upwards. Gravity ceased to exist. At the top of the loop shaped track, I could see for miles and miles. A hot air balloon floated just below my line of sight. Then, we curved straight downward and it felt like I was in a roadrunner cartoon, running straight down a cliff. We deccelerated and reached the platform, in a matter of what seemed like 2 seconds.

Joey unbuckled himself and started jumping around.

"That was lit af!"

My head was spinning. It took a lot out of me just to bring myself up out of the rocket seat on the coaster. I gathered myself and said, "alright, let's go find the girls and get outta here."

"Sounds like a plan, Stan."

Once we arrived back at the pool, we scanned the large crowd for Beth and Natalie. We walked from east to west, and couldn't find them anywhere. The wave pool was out of service, and people were packing up their things and getting ready to leave.

"Bro, I don't see them anywhere!"

"Me neither. Maybe they're walking out and we can meet them at the car."

"Good idea. I'll text Natalie and let her know."

I never heard back from Natalie, and we waited 20 minutes at the car, to no avail.

"What should we do, man? Go back in to look for them?"

I turned around in my seat, scanning the crowd for any sign of Beth's sunhat. Just then, the amusement park officials started closing the gates.

"Shit, bro. The park is closed. Where could they be?"

"Who knows. She still hasn't texted back?"

"Nah."

I sat there in silence for a minute, running through all the possibilities in my head. Could they have been hurt in the wave pool and taken to the hospital? Did they meet other guys and leave with them? Or were they locked inside the park?

"I don't know what to do, except maybe call them a few times."

"Good idea," Joey agreed.

No answer.

"Damn it. I can't believe this is happening."

Joey said, "dude, they probably called their parents to come get them or something."

"Maybe. I just hate feeling like we're leaving them stranded like this."

"Come on, man. I bet if we drove home, we'd see them at school on Monday."

I gave Joey a concerned look as I bit my fingernails, before saying, "OK. But if they text or call, we gotta turn around and come get them."

It was a strange drive home. The clouds seemed a lot more hazy. There were very few cars on the road. Joey and I didn't speak. We were too nervous to joke around and enjoy ourselves. As I turned off the highway into our exit just outside of Albuquerque, I noticed something odd. The exit sign was spray painted over. It wasn't like that the last time I passed that sign, just 2 days before. And when we drove down main street, all the shops were boarded up and graffitied over as well.

"Bro, what is going on right now?"

"I have no idea. This kinda creeps me out," Joey replied.

When we arrived back at my place, we jumped out of the car and walked up to the door. Locked. I circled around the porch to the garage, but the garage code didn't work. I tried calling my dad, he didn't even answer.

"Shit. I don't know what to do. My dad isn't answering. Can we go to your house?"

"Do we have any other option?"

But when we reached Joey's neighborhood on the south side, it was completely unrecognizable. The entrance was scattered with broken trees and busted up cars. Houses were torn apart, drywall and metal lay strewn over lawns like decorations. One house was even on fire. We didn't say a word. Our mouths hung open in disbelief as I maneuvered the car through the rubble on the street. I pulled up against the sidewalk in front of Joey's house, he got out and ran to the front door. It hung on by one hinge. He pushed it open and stepped inside. Nothing was in order. The couch was torn up, pictures and tables smashed to bits.

"Mom? Dad?" He called out. No answer. He ran through the kitchen and upstairs.

"Mom? Dad? Anyone here?" Dead silence. He ran back outside, appearing beyond spooked.

"Were they home?"

"No, dude. What the hell happened here?"

"Not sure, but we're gonna find out."

We got back in the car and began to exit the neighborhood. The place was devoid of life. We were scared shitless. Further down the road, a man in torn up clothes ran out into the road, waving us down. I slowed and rolled down my window.

"Please, you gotta help me. You're the only car I've seen in days!" The man pleaded.

"We were hoping you could help us," I answered. "What happened here?"

"Everything, man, where have you been? The riots, communist air strikes, nuclear meltdowns, political corruption, this place has been messed up this whole year!" He spat out, breathing heavily.

"What do you mean, this whole year? We've been gone half a day." I looked over at Joey, his expression shocked.

"Whatever, man. Can you help me please? I need a ride outta this town."

I rolled up the window and sped off down the road.

"Bro, what the hell is going on right now?" Joey panicked.

I steered through debris, asking myself the same exact thing. Then, it hit me.

"Oh shit! No, there's no freaking way."

"What!?" Joey coerced me.

"Well, do you think that, maybe by some small chance, that the Interstellar

Express was some kind of, time machine?"

Joey paused, then said, "damn. And what, we got sent into the future or something?"

"That's the only thing I can come up with."

Further down the road, we passed a bank with an electric sign in front. The date read September 27th, 2023. The ominous numbers stifled me. It was all so surreal. What were we gonna do? We had to get back to that amusement park, and travel back into the past to fix whatever caused this mess. So the next day, that's exactly what we did.

Chapter Six

"You are such a bitch Tara! I can't believe you posted that! Did you know that everyone is talking about me?" Donnie yelled.

Tara shrugged, clearly indifferent to what Donnie was upset about.

"If my dad finds out, he's gonna whoop my ass. What were you thinking?"

"I just wanted to show everyone how passionate we were about each other," she replied calmly.

"Passionate? We hung out one time. We shouldn't even be having this conversation. Delete the video or I'll tell the cops about your little underage porn scandal."

"You wouldn't! You'd be in just as much trouble!"

"Not really, you can't even tell it's me. Delete the video or else."

Tara stuck her tongue out like a little sissy and stomped away.

"I mean it!" Donnie shouted down the hallway.

Tara flipped a middle finger behind her.

At home, Donnie crashed down onto his couch and cracked a soda can. His dad made his way down the stairs, saw Donnie, and said, "hey champ! Good to see ya. Hey, I got some good news for ya."

"What is it?"

"So, one of the board members had their secretary fired, and they moved my personal consultant to another department. Which means, you can be hired on as my new helper!"

Donnie took a swig from his soda can and wiped his mouth with the back of his hand, then said, "dad, I appreciate the offer, but I don't want to get into politics."

"Why not? This is your big chance at a great career."

"Dad, I want to draw cartoons. I don't want to get swept up in some fiasco of a business. And besides, what the hell do I have to offer?"

"You can pour me coffee in the mornings! And run paperwork around."

"That sounds terrible!" Donnie remarked.

"Oh, and I forgot. You get to stand behind me on the podium when I'm giving speeches!"

Donnie considered the last statement for a moment, then said, "I don't know, dad. That's a big commitment. I wanna have time for myself."

"Donnie, you're taking the job. I'm not gonna let you fall into the same lifestyle that your brother did."

"James is nothing like me. He had zero talent."

"Well, he had plenty of opportunities, and I'm giving you an excellent one now. You're coming with me tomorrow to the office."

Donnie set his can down on the coffee table and kicked up his shoes next to it, placing his arms behind his head.

"And get your damn shoes off of my coffee table!"

Later that night, around 1 A.M., Donnie snuck out and hopped in his new car, then took off. He had no plan, he just wanted to go for a drive to clear his head. Donnie thought about the possible repercussions of taking this job, how far he would eventually fall down the political rabbit hole. He thought about the drama with Tara, how he was so happy when he was with her and how things turned on him 180 degrees. And what were people saying about him? Donnie had only one friend, and even Gib was giving him a hard time. Donnie felt like driving his new car was the only relief he could find during his inevitable coming of age. He wished he could go back to a simpler time. Escape the madness of reality.

Donnie fetched his usual blueberry waffles out of the freezer, and loaded them into the toaster. He sat down at the kitchen table, and pulled up Instagram on his phone. His dad entered the kitchen, and began digging through his briefcase to pull out a paper.

"This is the official job specifications and salary description. I'll be back at 3:30 to come get you." He closed his briefcase and grabbed his blazer off the rack. "And you will be dressed appropriately. No baggy jeans or graphic T-shirts. Got it?"

Donnie mumbled, not looking up from his phone. His dad walked out the door, and waffles shot out of the toaster. Donnie grabbed the syrup and butter out of the fridge. He smothered several spoons of butter on and drowned them with half the bottle of goo. A text popped up on his phone, from Gib. 'Meet me at the park in 5. Bring your board.'

The two of them skated for a solid 15 minutes, pulling olleys and grinding over metal poles. Donnie kicked up his board, and pulled out the paper his dad gave him.

"The pops wants me to take a job at the office," he said, handing Gib the paper.

"What's this?"

"The job description."

"100k per year! Dude, you know how much weed we could buy with that kind of cash?"

"I don't want the job."

"What? Why the hell not? Do you realize what kind of potential this has for our lives?"

"You keep bringing yourself up like this has something to do with you. It's always about you, Gib. How much weed you can smoke, how much video games you can play, piss off man." Donnie snatched the paper out of his hands and stuffed it back into his pocket.

"Bro, I'm just saying. With that kind of money, you wouldn't have a damn thing to worry about." Gib jumped back on his board and rolled away. "Can't draw cartoons for the rest of your life, man."

When 3:30 came around, Donnie was waiting in the living room, dressed in slacks and a polo. His dad showed up, and Donnie reluctantly left with his dad.

The two of them entered into the highly secured building where Jack worked, and winded through the hallways until they arrived at his office.

"Well, here's the contract and tax information. All you have to do is sign at the X and I'll fill out the rest," Jack informed his son.

Jack's desk intercom buzzed, and he pressed the button before answering, "yes, Martha?"

"Jack. We have an army general from the central Wyoming nuclear base here to see you."

"Send em up."

"Nuclear base, huh?" Donnie pondered.

"Yeah, we get a few of these yahoos in here every once in a while. Typically looking for an extra stimulus package so them and their boys can pop off more rounds at the range or something," Jack responded smoothly, like he knew what the hell he was talking about.

Donnie signed the X and slided the paper back towards his dad. "So what else do you do in here besides play games on your computer?" Donnie joked.

"Donnie, I'm the speaker of the house. I rarely have time to check my own email, let alone play computer games. Maybe you've confused me for one of your lousy ass teachers."

Right then, the army general plowed through the door and into Jack's office. He straightened himself, saluted, and seated himself next to Donnie. "Who's this kid?"

"That's my son, Donnie. He's going to be filling in as my new secretary," Jack explained.

"Looks like he just graduated middle school."

"Yeah, right. And your name is?"

"General David Swellwater. I've come here on short notice to discuss top secret information."

"Continue," Jack suggested, picking up a pen from his desk and twirling it around his fingers.

"Using our new advanced satellites, our boys out in Wyoming were able to detect a signal traveling from a distant object some 2 light years away. It seems that the United States of America is the first country on Earth to have received contact from an extraterrestrial civilization, Jack."

"Holy smokes. What did they say?"

"Who the hell knows. Could've meant anything."

"And are they traveling towards us?"

"I believe so."

"How fast?"

"By our estimation, they should reach our planet in three and a half years."

"This is ground-breaking. How are we gonna inform the American public?" Jack quizzed him.

"We won't."

Jack, baffled at the previous statement, coughed and said, "well why the hell not? Don't they deserve to know?"

"Not if they never reach us."

"So what? You're gonna blast these aliens right out of existence?"

"Pretty much."

Donnie sat with his eyes wide and eyebrows wrinkled.

"What if they have something valuable to offer us?"

The general hummed, scratched his head, and said, "y'know, we never considered that. I'm gonna get in contact with my superiors and reconsider our approach. Catch ya later, Jack," he said before standing out of his chair.

"Ooh, are these jelly filled?" He asked before snatching a donut off of Jack's desk and chomping down hard, spilling grape goo all over Donnie's contract and leaving the office.

"What did I tell ya? These army guys are about as sharp as butter knives," Jack joked with Donnie.

The two of them spent most of the day tossing a football back and forth across the office, listening to rock music and watching television. Until Martha buzzed in on Jack's intercom.

"Jack?"

"What is it, Martha?"

"We have a lady here from the school district. Says she needs to speak with you about funding."

Jack sighed and said, "send her up."

The elderly woman turned the handle on the door, but could not for the life of her push hard enough *and* balance herself on her cane to get it open. Donnie jumped out of his seat and opened it for her.

"Thank you, young man."

She inched her way over to the extra chair, and settled herself down as slowly as possible.

"Welcome to my office! I'm Jack Williams, speaker of the-"

"Yeah, I know who you are, good-for-nothing son of a bitch," she cringed.

"I- I'm sorry? And who are you?"

"My name is Janice Weatherfield, executive chairwoman of District of Columbia Public Schools. I'm here to have a little chat with you about fund decreases this year and last."

"Mhmm, I see. And what is it you wanted to discuss about those fund cuts?" Jack wondered out loud.

"They're unacceptable! Our classrooms have become jungle gyms! Kids can't read, write, or use computers! And it all comes back to you, Jack Williams," she snarled.

"Ma'am, first of all, I just recently became the speaker of the house not two weeks ago. Second of all, the speaker of the house has nothing to do with the total vote count or the manner in which your school district disburses those funds," he corrected her.

"Oh fooey! You know, those kids deserve the same chance you did growing up. Maybe you should try showing a little compassion to them, it would go a long way towards fixing this screwed up country," Janice reprimanded Jack before making the strenuous effort of climbing up out of her chair and struggling back towards the office door.

"Donnie, can you grab the-"

"You've done enough already, Jack. Put a sock in it!" Janice screamed. She barely managed to crack the door open, before sliding her cane in the crevice and propping the door open just enough to make her way out.

Jack looked at Donnie, shrugged, and tossed the football back over his desk.

Over the course of the next few days at the office, nothing special happened. Donnie, run and get me a coffee. Donnie, get some copies made. Donnie, scrub the toilets. Except for one day, Jack ordered two pizzas up to his office, and his secretary, Martha, accidentally sent them to someone else.

Jack waited two hours before finally buzzing down to see what was going on.

"Martha, have you seen my two pizzas yet? They should be here by now."

"Oh! Um, They'll be right up sir!" Martha rushed to the office she sent them to, but didn't get there in time. The politicians were already halfway through the second box. *Shit,* she mumbled to herself.

"Um, Jack?"

"Yes, Martha."

"Slight mix-up. I accidentally sent those pizzas up to another office."

"You did what!? You're fired! Pack your shit, Martha!"

"But sir, I can just order a new-"

"I said you're fired!"

Later the next week, Jack had an actual speech to make, and Donnie tagged along with him. Donnie was excited. It was going to be his first time on national television. He knew this was going to make up for all the slander surrounding him at school. What Donnie didn't know was that the repercussions of his father's speech would set off a wild chain reaction of events.

"Fellow Americans. I stand in front of you today amidst a crisis. For the first time in the history of our country, we have a severe oil shortage on our hands," he began.

The audience grew tense as Jack shuffled his papers atop the podium.

"The energy we normally receive from coal and solar panels has dropped

30 percent. Wind turbines have become significantly more expensive to produce. The middle east has found a way to pull the rug out from under us. But there is no reason to fret. The Board of Energy has come up with a fairly felicitous solution to our problem. We have just approved the construction of a series of super-sized nuclear power plants, effectively nullifying the middle east's attempt to vitiate our growth as a nation. Our total energy production will soon become irrepressible enough to support the entire planet."

Applause breaks out amongst the spectators, and Donnie pats his father on the back. The noise dies down, and Jack concludes his speech.

"To put things in perspective, we believe with this new energy-surplus, the global economy will become dirigible enough in our favor to wipe out the national debt before 2030!"

The crowd roars and Jacks waves as he exits the platform with Donnie and his security guards.

Chapter Seven

Joey and I drove back over to my place, an empty shell of what was once a home, to stay the night before attempting our journey back to the year 2020. During the drive home, I felt a fleeting moment of joy as I reminisced on some of my younger days, when my mother was still around. She would invite a few family friends over, and we would play Rockband on our PS2. I vividly recall jamming out to "When You Were Young" by The Killers, either drumming away on the make-shift drum set or strumming series of colored notes on the guitar.

We arrived at my place, and I locked up the whip before we dragged ourselves into the house. We were worn out.

"Want any food?" I asked Joey.

"Is there any here?"

"Let's check."

I flicked the switch on in the kitchen, but the power was out.

"Damnit. Looks like we gotta use our phones."

I turned on my flashlight, and rummaged through the cabinets and pantry, with no sign of any grub. The fridge was empty, except for some moldy cottage cheese.

"Sorry man. I would say let's order in, but I doubt any place would be delivering after a nuclear fallout."

"Yeah, great analysis captain jackass," Joey murmured.

"Cut the shit, you smelly douche canoe. We've gotta get some rest before tomorrow."

That night, I replayed another fond memory from my childhood. I remember every night, when I was maybe six or seven, my mother used to prop herself against the edge of my bed and read Harry Potter books to me before I went to sleep. She genuinely wanted me to be happy, I could tell. All the little things she did for me helped me appreciate life on another level. I'll never forget how special she made me feel.

The next morning, we awoke with rumbling stomachs and headaches. Joey and I hopped in the car, and headed for Desert Flags.

"We should stop and grab some food on the way there," Joey proposed.

"Oh yeah? And where would you like to go?"

"I say we pay a visit to one of those seven elevens and stash all we can fit into this gym bag of yours."

"I'm game."

We pulled up to a closed down convenience store, and walked up to find the expected, a locked door with a sign in the window, which read 'closed due to apocalypse. We apologize for any inconvenience'.

Joey blurted out, "oh, how polite!" And then took the blunt end of his pocket knife and smashed through the glass door, casually stepping inside.

"What? Never broke into a store before?"

We ended up filling a whole garbage bag full of snacks and drinks before making our departure. Joey flipped on the radio and Michael Jackson's "Smooth Criminal" was playing on 97.7 the Zing.

We entered the Desert Flags parking lot, shocked to find no cars and a locked off entrance.

"What the hell? This place was a damn circus yesterday!"

I stared at the gate, puzzled myself. "Well, maybe there was some kind of buffer zone after we traveled into the future."

"Maybe. We're gonna have to hop the gate and operate the Interstellar Express ourselves," Joey announced.

We made it over no problem. The inside was vacant, with tumble weeds scattered across the area where the wave pool used to teem with cheerful swimmers.

"This is creepy as hell," Joey staggered.

"This is hell. We need to get back to 2020 and stop this from ever happening," I reminded him.

We reached the Interstellar Express, and were glad to see the lights and motors start up when I flipped the power switch.

"All aboard!" Joey called out through clasped hands.

"This is no time for jokes, dicknose. Now help me figure out where I can configure the time destination."

"Check under the control panel."

"Where?"

"The metal podium where you flicked the power switch? Try opening the door underneath."

I yanked it open, and was exhilarated to find a glowing time dial with a lever to select the desired time destination.

"It's in here! Joey you're a freaking genius!"

"I know. Now fire this baby up and get us outta here."

I selected September 17th, 2020, the day we left. Then, I hastily climbed into the alien-themed rocket ship and strapped myself in.

"Oh shit!"

"What is it?" Joey asked me.

"How are we gonna press the green button if we're already strapped in?"

Joey rolled his eyes, and said, "I got this."

He took off his other shoe, and tossed a perfect lob directly at the green button, punching in our freedom.

"Savage, bro."

Within seconds, the coaster blasted away from the platform, sending us flying towards the sky once again on the loop shaped track. When we arrived back at the platform, we were relieved to see there was a large crowd waiting by the roller coaster. We got off the ride and set our sights in the direction of the wave pool.

We found Natalie and Bethany lounging in two of the beach chairs.

"It's about time you guys showed up!" Beth declared.

"Sorry, we took a little detour," Joey responded.

"Yeah, whatever. We're ready to leave when you are."

So, we pulled our stuff together and walked out to the car like we didn't just time travel. We had no intention of disclosing the previous events because we were afraid they wouldn't want to hangout with us again, or that word would get out about the time traveling coaster.

When we pulled into town, I was so excited to see that the place was back to normal. To celebrate our adventure, I pulled into a vacant parking lot and started burning donuts in my dad's beamer. The girls screamed from the backseat, holding on for dear life to the roof handles. Joey hung out the window, the wind whipping his hair as he hollered. I flipped around and started burning donuts in the other direction, but one of them got out of control and I tried hitting the brakes, but couldn't stop the left bumper corner from clipping a pole at the edge of the lot. The car skidded to a halt and I jumped out the driver's door.

I stood, hands on my head, staring in disbelief at the damage. Joey got out and stood next to me, and placed a hand on my shoulder.

"My dad is gonna send me to military camp. Lock me in the basement. Chain me to a wooden chair and kick it over so I can't-"

"Marco, calm down, man. Just chill. Your dad is not gonna-"

"You don't know my dad, Joey."

"Well, shit, man. Just say somebody rear ended you on the way home from the park."

"Yeah, and then he'll ask me for their insurance information, dumbass."

"Just say it was a hit and run. Nothing you could do about it."

I stood there for a moment, considering the possible consequences.

"I guess that will work."

"Of course it will. Now, we gotta deal with the girls, bro. Keep them from telling their parents."

"Damn, you're right."

"I'm always right."

Joey and I carefully climbed back into the car, and slammed the doors shut before I drove off. Joey turned around and said, "OK, here's the deal. You don't tell your parents about this, and we buy you lunch for the rest of the school year."

"Joey!" I said.

"Shhh, calm down, Ricky Bobby."

The girls giggled and agreed to our deal.

I dropped everybody off, and pulled into my driveway. I saw my dad inside, cooking dinner, and got a strange feeling in my stomach.

"Umm, dad?"

"Oh, hey! There you are! How was the carnival?"

"Dad, we went to the amusement park."

"Ah, same thing."

"It was pretty cool. We rode some rides, swam in the pool, one of the girls got sick and puked off the Tower of Zoom."

"No kidding, huh? What, too much funnel cake?"

"I guess."

My dad walked over with the skillet and dumped some hash browns on my plate.

"Want any hot sauce?"

"Sure."

He pulled the tobasco out of the fridge and set it down in front of me before plopping down in his chair.

"Dad?"

"What is it, sporto?"

"There's something I have to tell you."

He gave me an odd look before saying, "what's up?"

"On the way back home. Somebody hit the back of your car."

He set his fork down and stopped chewing his food. "Are you serious? Did you guys stop and exchange info?"

I hesitated, then said, "well, no. He drove away before we could do anything."

"That's unacceptable! Marco, you're grounded! No more video games, no more TV, no more going outside! I don't care if Santa Claus is selling tacos on the corner!"

I sat there with my mouth hanging open.

He looked at me square in the eyes, then said, "just kidding. Gotcha that time!" and started cracking up.

"Wha-?"

"That wasn't your fault! You need to learn how to be easier on yourself, man! Lighten up!"

"But what about the car?"

"Marco, I rake in 700k a year. I could buy ten of them."

After dinner, I walked upstairs and flopped down onto my bed. I flipped on my TV, and started channel surfing. I saw something that caught my eye. It looked like a huge press conference airing live on the news channel, a man up behind the podium with cameras flashing and a banner that read 'BREAKING NEWS: Jack Williams announces plans to open giant nuclear plant in the heart of D.C.' I thought back to what that Coyote Bongwater guy had told me, and started piecing things together. The nuclear fallout me and Joey saw, the timing of our adventure, the controversy with police brutality. I needed to do something. But what?

Chapter Eight

Donnie knew what his father and government were doing was wrong. He knew damn well that a giant new nuclear power plant and provisions to enforce martial law were beyond dangerous, even unethical. But he didn't care. He liked his newfound power, a little too much. Kids at school studied him with fear in their hearts, fully aware that he had a prosperous and influential life ahead of him, and they would be forced to settle for the average cycle of minimum fulfillment. Donnie swaggered around the halls as if he were untouchable, and even Gib was surprised to see Donnie like this the next time they crossed paths.

"What's up, bro?" Gib asked, timidly.

"Busy. Homework, girls, helping out at the office."

"Girls? Office? Check out big dog over here!"

Donnie glanced at Gib indifferently before brushing past him on the way to his new car.

"Hey, wait up broseph!"

Donnie waved him off and continued through the rugged hallway of Pioneer Memorial High.

Donnie no longer had time for the trivial ways of Gib and the adolescent lifestyle. He was a powerful politician, or at least the secretary for one. There were more important things to attend to.

Donnie arrived at the office around 3:45, dressed to the nines and ready for some serious lounging around.

"Donnie! Good to see ya," one of his father's associates greeted him. Donnie offered him a sly smirk and walked right past him.

"Hey, honeybun. Glad you're here," Martha cheerfully remarked.

Donnie gave her the snap-and-point, then winked at her as if he was implying certain relations in the near future. She blushed and raked her hair with her fingers.

Donnie breezed through the door to his dad's office, gave him a nod, and sat back into the chair facing his desk.

"Big day ahead of us," his dad began. "Lots of paperwork and bathroom cleaning to take care of."

"Really? Don't you have anything better for me to do?"

"What's the problem? This is the foundation, Donnie. You have to lay the foundation before you just go driving support beams into the ground."

Donnie sighed, and said, "yeah, I get that. But I'm big time pops. I need responsibility, power."

"Ok, Mr. big time. How about this. Take your sophisticated ass over to the coffee machine, and pour me out a big time cup a joe. Sound good?"

Donnie scoffed, rolled his eyes, and stood out of his chair and walked out the door.

Walking through the hall, not making any sort of progress towards the break room, Donnie scanned his phone while nonchalantly swinging his lanyard in circles around his pointer finger. He tentatively turned the corner, looked both ways, nobody there. Still scrolling through his Twitter feed, he nearly ran straight into a tall brunette woman strutting in her high heels.

"My bad," Donnie said.

She sidestepped him, and scanned him up and down before saying, "my, my. Lucky for you, bad is how I like them."

Donnie chuckled and stuffed his phone in his pocket before leaning casually against the wall.

"Well aren't you a foxy mama."

She smiled and stepped closer to him. He curled his hand around the small of her back and pulled her closer. Their lips came together gently, before the heat cranked up. They grabbed each other all over and soon found themselves pulling off eachother's clothes in a dark closet.

"What the hell took you so long?"

"I took a little detour."

"Where's my damn coffee?"

"Oh, right. Forgot. I'll be right back."

"No! Sit your ass down!"

Donnie cautiously sat back down in his chair.

Jack twiddled his thumbs, looking from his computer to Donnie through square glasses. Back to his computer, then back to Donnie. One more time at his computer. He vibrated air through closed lips, as if he were blowing away stress. He unfolded his hands, placed them flat against his desk, and pushed himself up from his chair and walked towards the whiteboard in his office. He grabbed a green marker from the metal shelf, popped the cap off, and started drawing a venn diagram.

"Donnie," he began. "This side represents you," he explained, writing Donnie's name above the right circle. "This side represents me," he said, writing 'Me' above the left circle. "And the middle represents the things we share in common."

"Dad, I know what a venn diagram is."

"Quiet!" Jack commenced jotting down characteristics in Donnie's circle. Lazy. Superficial. Pompous. Unfocused. Materialistic. Precarious. Under his name, he wrote down traits he felt expressed himself. Driven. Powerful. Sophisticated. Mature. In the middle, he wrote 'we live in the same house'.

"Wow," Donnie said sarcastically.

"Does any of this ring a bell?" Jack snapped the cap back on his green white board marker, and set it back on the shelf. "Donnie, at some point in your life, you're going to realize that it's all about the little things. How you present yourself, the people you have around you. That friend of yours, Gib? He's obviously missing a few tools from his toolbox. Is that the kind of person you want to be like Donnie?"

Donnie crossed his arms, pouting. "No."

"That's what I thought. Now take your lethargic ass over to the break room, and pour me a damn coffee!"

Donnie stood and yanked open the door.

"Three sugar packets! Three!"

Frustrated with his experience at the office that day, Donnie got in his Cadillac and drove to Booze n' Cruise, a local liquor store. Using a fake ID he got from a website, he bought a six pack and cracked open a bottle as he was pulling away. He downed at least four on his way back home, zooming past people with his middle finger out the window. He slammed on his brakes skidding over his front lawn, and parked sideways on the street.

"Whoops!" Donnie exclaimed, observing his black tire marks on the grass while sauntering up to the front door.

Inside, he tumbled down onto the couch, and pulled his notebook out from under the coffee table. "Wait til the D.C. Tabbernazzle gets a load of this one," Donnie quipped.

"This is libel! An utter misrepresentation!" Jack Williams complained to Martha, standing awkwardly in his office while he jabbed a finger into the newspaper.

"Jack. How bad can it be?"

"Take a look for yourself! 70 million people read the Tabbernazzle every week, Martha. 70. Million."

Martha took one brief look at the cartoon, and placed a hand over her mouth in an attempt to hide her laugh.

"I'm sorry, Jack. I'm so, very sorry." She rushed out of his office and closed the door.

Jack rested his elbows on his desk, and dropped his head down in defeat. The cartoon, drawn by an anonymous artist, displayed Jack as a puppet on the podium, being controlled by an arm extending from a curtain. His dialogue read, 'these new state-of-the art power plants are almost as radioactive as my fallacious self confidence!'

Chapter Nine

Over the weekend, I took a walk, ruminating over the previous journey and speech I watched on TV. I changed the song on my playlist, and looked over to my left as I passed an exotic sports car dealership. I noticed a black Lamborghini Mercy, and couldn't resist walking up for a closer examination. I took a snapchat, and ran my hand along the smooth metal exterior as I walked around the side. I tapped the roof a couple times, before the dealer blasted through the front door.

"Don't touch my car!"

A crooked grin grew gradually over my face, and I said, "I am a Lamborghini."

"Get the hell out of here!"

"Suck this dick, faggot."

The dealer, several inches taller, and about 40 pounds heavier than me, chased me out of the lot.

"You come back here and I beat your ass!"

"God bless," I beamed.

The next day, I suited up and traveled with my dad to a baseball game. I was the starting pitcher that day, a challenge awaiting me in the T&C Fireballs. As I took the mound, the sun bounced vibrantly off of the number seven, laminated across the back of my purple New Mexico Magic jersey.

It was late in the final inning. The Magic were slightly ahead of the Fireballs, 1-0. The Fireballs were the home team, so they had last bats while I went for the no-hitter. I took the mound with conviction, and ended up walking the first three batters. My dad called time, and jogged out for a meeting. My team started running in, and my dad waved them off. He arrived at the clump of dirt in the middle of the field, and took his cap off and slapped his knee before straightening it back on his head.

"Marco. Listen to me."

I kicked at the dirt with my cleat before looking up into his sunglasses.

"You've got a chance to make history here today. I don't know if you were aware, but you're pitching a no hitter right now. Now, I know I'm not supposed to mention that before it happens, but neither you nor I can afford to blow this one."

"This guy isn't giving me anything! I keep hitting the outside corner and he won't call it!"

My dad sighed, turned to look at the umpire, then placed both hands on my shoulders and said, "then throw it so good he *has* to call it," then jogged back to the dugout.

I kicked dirt back into the hole in front of the rubber, and rubbed some spit onto the dry leather of the baseball. I kicked into my wind-up, and fired a fastball. Ball 1. The Magic fans booed loudly, and I caught the ball back from my catcher. I wound up, and threw a change up for the second pitch. Ball 2.

"Marco! Pull your head out of your freaking ass, and throw a strike!" My dad yelled at me from the dugout.

I caught the ball, and took a deep breath in as I readjusted my belt. I stepped back onto the rubber, and nodded as I got the sign from my catcher. I kicked high, and threw a sinker, just barely missing the bottom of the zone, but skipping in the dirt past my catcher. I broke for the plate and caught the ball from my catcher who retrieved it from the backstop, bringing my mitt down just in time to tag the runner from third base out. Magic fans roared with applause, and I brushed dirt off my shoulder as I swaggered back to the mound.

I looked over at my dad, and he crossed his arms and shook his head. Nervously, I wound up and threw a fastball, missing the top of the zone. My catcher had to leave his feet in order to catch my wild pitch.

"Marco! Let's go!" My dad protested. Fans groaned and fanned themselves in the scorching summer heat. 1 out, bases loaded. A new batter approached the plate, and pointed his bat for the left field fence, predicting a home run. Magic fans booed.

I slowly went into the motion of my wind up, and sent a fastball directly down the middle of the strike zone. The batter slapped the shit out of the ball, sending a line drive right for my head. I quickly ducked, and stuck my mitt upwards in a faint attempt to catch the ball. By some dumb luck, The ball landed snug in my glove as I tumbled to the dirt. I jumped right up, and noticed that the runner on third was half way between his base and home plate. I slung the ball over to my third baseman, and the ball game was over. The no hitter was complete. My team stormed the mound, and lifted me up on their shoulders, Magic fans stood and exploded in applause as they carried me off the field.

"So what are you gonna do about this whole impending doom situation?" Joey quizzed me over the phone.

"I think I'm gonna write a paper, or start a boycott, something like that," I hypothesized.

"Oh yeah? You gonna get all educational and shit?"

"Joey, you can be a real shart socket, you know that?"

Joey laughed, and replied, "hey, by the way, I came up with another idea for a commercial in advertisment tech class. Wanna hear it?"

I sighed, and asked, "do I have a choice?"

"Okay, here it goes. The camera shows a physics teacher in class, explaining some type of law of nature. The narrator says, 'what this guy tells you in here, won't limit what we do out here.' The camera then shows a massive truck hauling a giant rock with a chain, directly up a 90 degree angle on a mountain. The narrator says, 'introducing the Ford F-750. With a V-32 engine and turbo thrusters, there's no stopping this force of nature."

"Joey, in what context is that even relevant?"

"Every context."

Later the next day, instead of basking in the success of yesterday, I sat down in front of my computer and wrote a paper concerning the energy crisis, police corruption, and possible solutions.

I explained that utilizing knowledge gained from quantum physics and the baryon-annihilation process, we could safely convert matter into unlimited energy using electrowear tunneling, effectively reducing Earth's pollution to zero. I touched base on epigenetics, specifically, how the way you see yourself can actually change your DNA structure for better or worse. I proposed the installment of a new law enforcement agency, called the 'X-Police'. They could patrol the streets, and make sure that people were not being wrongly mistreated by the regular police. Furthermore, I mentioned the Cosmological Singularity, a force that exists outside of space and time, which alreadys knows how the universe will end and acts as an invisible hand to keep life from destroying itself. I sent my finished paper into a scientific journal, and the next day, it was published for millions of readers to see.

Afterwards, I traveled around the city and posted papers inviting people to join me in a boycott of cars, relying solely on travel by bicycle. I advertised on social media as well, and my movement gained a mass following seemingly overnight. Pretty soon, the entire country was riding a bike to work.

"Marco, I read your paper and saw your boycott stuff. I think it's pretty cool," Natalie said to me one day in the hallway.

"Oh really? Yeah, I just wanted to do something positive for the planet, especially while I'm still so young."

Natalie bit her lip and smiled, before saying, "I think being smart is pretty sexy."

Taken back from her statement, I gathered myself to say, "oh is that so? You know, procrastination is a deadly sin," winking at her.

"What are you getting at, Mark?"

"Y'know, I just think, it's better to get your feelings out in the open before it's too late. And, I've been meaning to ask you on a date for a while. So, Natalie, do you wanna grab some coffee sometime?"

“That sounds great.”

www.ingramcontent.com/pod-product-compliance
Lightning Source LLC
LaVergne TN
LVHW041033150826
845672LV00001B/306

9798663453226